I Ain't Misbehavin'

By Curtis R. Crim

ISBN: 978-0-9888255-2-9

Printed in the United States of America

First Printing

For Anna

TABLE OF CUNTENTS

Preface

I have always had a very strange mind. I don't claim to have thought processes that resemble that of a normal human being. My mind is in fact so bizarre, that I have managed on rare occasions to come up with some of the sickest and most fucked-up thoughts in history (if you don't believe me, then read _Auschwitz: A Love Story,_ by yours truly (hehehe…).

As I work my organic farm, make pottery from the clay I dig up, and tend my bees, I find my mind straying into unusual places, and sometimes coming up with some really funny thoughts! I am 50 years old now, and can only manage to remember about three jokes until I get to a computer to write them down. ☹ This year, I think that I only remembered about one out of every three jokes that came to me while I was out working. This book is the sequel to my first book of jokes, _I Aim to Misbehave_.

As with any collection of humor, the average reader will find some of my jokes really funny, some worth only a little snicker, and some downright offensive. I don't expect any two readers to react the same way to my off-beat and freaky humor.

So with no further adieu, I hope that you get at least a few laughs out of the following pages. ☺

-Curtis R. Crim

Chapter 1: One-Liners

I hate getting beat up, so I never fight with anyone over the age of two.

I call my brother in law "Tom Tom, the Piper's Son", because he stole a pig.

When physicists hug, do quantum realities collide?

Is it two and a half *men*, or two and a half *inches*?

Did you know that if you are Iowan, you are considered mentally disabled by the Federal Government?

Well, maybe I didn't fall off my diet last night, but I didn't fall *on* it either!

Keep your friends close, and your girlfriends closer!

You are *really* pathetic when you get rejected by a NON-human animal!

Can there be a connoisseur of connoisseurs?

I fear being left alone with myself, because I am afraid of getting molested, and that I will be helpless to stop it.

I wasn't barking up the wrong tree; I was barking up the wrong sprout!

Can a person be a trans-dimensional cross-dresser?

Playing Michael Jackson on a rock and roll station is like praying to Satan in a Christian church!

Pooing is your primary doodie in life.

Just because I don't have a job doesn't mean that I can't take some time off!

The only thing I have been absolutely sure of is how confused I am!

A near miss is better than no miss at all.

Today, I won a HUGE victory over a very, very small moth.

If you are a man who is loved by women, then you get pussy, if not, then you get cats.

I love babies because they fit nicely into a stockpot.

Have you ever belched like you are angry?

I sometimes wonder if I am just weeding something into it.

I "took one for the team", and then found out that it was the *wrong team*!

My only relationship is with myself; however, we've been having a *lot* of sex lately!

We have plenty of mead, honey.

Cry havoc, and set loose the lemmings of war!

Women think that I am a terrible lover, but even as a gay, I suck!

Who came first, the chicken or the farmer?

It is a *really **bad*** idea to give hallucinogens to a cat!

I think that virgins are FUCKING BASTARDS!

I am sorry that you are getting older, but do you have to be so *retarded* about being senile?

You can go to realdoll.com and pick up a woman who is entirely silicone, or you can go to Hollywood and pick up one is *really close.*

Well, if you are as much like me as I am…

A girlfriend once asked me if I some day wanted to have kids. I am like, "Duh!" They are like, *super* limber!

Just go ahead and *try* to burn an e-Book!

Never kill a fly on the window with a hammer.

I haven't really *lost* weight; it's just *archived.*

Cats and blow-up furniture don't mix...

I am sorry, but I don't really consider myself to be a mature audience!

Women are *collectively* a CUNT!

Are bestialist matchmakers into animal husbandry?

When I see a hot chick eating pizza, it's like seeing my favorite thing in the world eating my other favorite thing in the world.

What's the difference between a shamrock and a real one?

My wife *desperately* wanted children to yell at.

Delta dong, what's that power you have on?

The feeding is not over until the fat kitty mings.

I am sometimes antisocial towards myself.

So which *is* more dangerous, a food processor or a word processor?

For my ex-wife, anger was a pre-requisite for consciousness.

Ever fart so bad that you offended yourself?

I'm not just laughing with myself; I am laughing *at* myself!

When a group of cats socially excommunicates one individual cat, it is known as "purrsecution".

Stupid people have smart phones.

My cat pussy-farted on me.

I got much more popular when I lost all of my teeth.

Being superficial is a terrible waste of pussy!

When my dog wants me to play with him, I have to do it, or he will just play with himself.

Are Sicilian women born angry?

Bees are carboholics.

When people build barriers around themselves, I find it very a-fence-ive.

Have you ever noticed that it is impossible to type while you are sneezing?

I am androgynous, but I only date hermaphrodites.

See that rooster over there? He is a real cock!

Is "testosteroni" a kind of pasta?

Pussy is very difficult to *come* by.

Having children is a childish thing to do.

It is harder to get it on than it is to get it off.

What the fuck is a *car toad* anyway?

There are some hard blow legs in the fridge.

Bad grammar just *sounds* better in a rural accent…

They might be *pussies,* but they are also such *dicks!*

Revenge is self-defense with lag.

I experienced a BBQ epiphany.

At BEST you are only *50%* of a relationship!

If you *do* grab a plastic shopping bag in the presence of a cat, do it slowly!

You know it's springtime when the *rednecks* start acting like it is spring time.

I *like* pussy; I just don't like what comes inside it.

So I finally met "little miss angry" and I married her.

When bunnies live together, it is known as "co-rabbitation".

More than one out of every 10 American women will admit to having ridden a bull, but none will admit to having had sex with me...

I asked for an exorcist and they brought me Gene Simmons...

My ex-wife always acted like someone shoved two fighting cats up her ass!

Being an old lady is better than not being a lady at all.

The sewage industry: now that's a load of shit!

Well looking masculine never got *me* laid!

It has been a long time since I have even kissed a *chicken!*

Cereal killers are what grasses fear!

I want pussy so badly that I can TASTE IT!

I once dated a woman who claimed that *both* of her parents died in child birth!

I tell my cat, "Think *inside* the box!"

It's easier to work the hose when it warms up.

My fish is a total hypochondriac!

You know what they say, a washed pot never boils.

My chickens are impeckable.

I find making nude friends hard to do.

It is hard to find a meaningful spiritual
relationship based on rape.

Chapter 2: Two Line Jokes

My nephew is 15 and has never shown interest in female humans. He is either going to be a monk, or a priest, if you know what I mean!

My ex-wife's Yorky could pee in many places. However, outside wasn't one of them!

When I see mud on my hen's back, I know that she has been mounted. When I see sperm on my girlfriend's back, I come to the same conclusion.

Ever puke on your computer keyboard? Most parts are edible.

They say don't count your chickens until they have hatched. My mother starts counting chickens while the rooster is still on top of the hen!

No officer; I am *not* a necrophiliac! I could see that she was old, but I *thought* that she was among the living!

In Iowa your mom and your aunt can be the same person. Saves money when buying Christmas gifts.

I asked this chick out and she turned me down; she said that she was married. I figured that she was probably lying, because she was ten…

Farmer's Wife: "Shit! The turkey is bleeding all over the place!"
Farmer: "I didn't even know that it was a girl!"

Friend: "Why is your wife so mad?"
Me: "She needs a reason?"

I was sitting on the john crapping when my manure delivery arrived. The irony was almost too much for me.

Dumbass Jehovahs Witness: "Is Jesus in your house?"
Me <gesturing behind me>: "He's out back in the dog shed."

What the *fuck* do you mean? I am never going to do something I have never done before *for the first time!*

I am as busy as a beaver! And we all know how much beavers like to get busy…

"My penis is shaped like a hot dog."
"Well that's some pretty frank talk!"

Vegetarians are no better than carnivores. Juice is the blood of plants.

I know that I am totally full of shit! It's okay, though; my condition is improving.

Dude: "Are you at least going to cook that shit before you eat it?"
Friend: "You know what they say: '*Only the good fry dung!*'"

Attorneys are like hookers. They both get people off.

Of course I hate that fucking cunt! She's *w*horeable.

My wife cheats on me once a month, always at the same time. I call it her, "Whore moanal fucktuation."

Sometimes, geniuses do the *stupidest* things! This is because they are creative, and unafraid to make mistakes.

Dude's Asshole: "Faaaarrrt!"
Dude's Buddy's Asshole: "I heard that!"

Strangely enough, my penis and I are attached right at the base of my dick. Therefore, if you take him on a trip, I am coming too!

I like runway models because they are *so* skinny that I think they need to eat something. But please, let me fuck her *first*!

It's not like I *want* to be a bad person. I think of it not so much as a curse but rather more like a gift…

I lost my wife eight years ago. It's okay. I know where she is; she's just not my wife anymore.

Well, I agree with Elton John in some ways. Don't let the son go down on me, but certainly *do* let Kate Beckinsale do it!

EVERY vote is a vote for George W. Bush. After all, he stole the presidency, and he's *not giving it back!*

I never read ANYTHING that I didn't write. That is because I don't trust anyone but myself to say anything that I want to hear!

My place is a steaming pile of manure. This is true on SO many different levels!

Bald guys are cocks. Have you ever seen a penis with hair on the end?

I have heard that medical doctors take an oath to not do any harm. Have you actually *seen* the bill?

They found a mad cow in Iowa…   Then I divorced her.

My mother is senile. Her brain has become a vestigial organ.

You rarely see anything pretty, white, and clean on my farm. Like my kitchen counter!

Chapter 3: Question & Answer Jokes

Q: What kind of snake can you eat with your food?
A: Anaconda-mints.

Q: How many dead judges does it take to change a light bulb?
A: It doesn't matter - just roll him over and I'll fuck him in the ass!

Question: How do you think that God created the universe?
Answer: He had the time.
Therefore: God created Time before it created *space*!

Q: How many geriatric people does it take to change a light bulb?
A: It isn't going to happen - the light's out, but nobody's home!

Chapter 4: Short Jokes

I used to have a girlfriend who had this awesome cat. She dumped me and it took me two years to get over her. It has been more than twenty five years now, and I still love her pussy!

Parent: "Here is your money. Where are my kids?"
Sitter: "They are visiting the people from New Guinea next door. It smells like they are cooking up something *really good* for dinner!"

This guy called me a son of a bitch. I was like, "You know my mother?"
And he's like, "Not since Sunday."

I hear that the US Marines are looking for a few good men. I also hear that a good man is hard to find. That's because of the camouflage.

I crap myself in the most cavalier manner. I do it *knightly*. You know, like Kiera.

I live on an organic farm, so I do a LOT of recycling. Anything that I am throwing out from the kitchen either gets composted or goes to livestock. The only thing that is wasted around here regularly is *me*!

Doctor: "I am so sorry to tell you the test results! You have malignant cancer, and you have about four months to live."
Patient: "At least I can fire my dentist!"

My ex-wife used to *hate* my pets! I have a fuzzy cat who she said was "the Devil". Well, all I can conclude is that if a fuzzy little cat is Satan, the God must really be a pussy!

I caught myself talking to myself *about* myself! Since I was doing right in front of me, I was failing to take *my* feelings into account...

They always talk about how many Jews Hitler killed. Here is the question that I want answered: How many *didn't* he?

Cats have nowhere *near* the social proprieties that we humans do. When a female cat goes into heat, it's *always* a gang-bang. I guess that's why they call it pussy!

I don't mind dating old women. It doesn't bother me at all. In fact, I have dated gals over ten, but it is much harder for me to force myself on them.

My sister and her high school boyfriend were very pro-life. They had an abortion together. I am not sure whether they named it...

If I have to fuck a woman's panties *into* her vagina, then that is exactly what I will do. If she doesn't like it, then perhaps the panties should have come off at about the same time the rest of her clothes did!

I have heard a lot about the Catholic priesthood and improprieties with small boys in the media lately. Well this is what I have to say about it: Pope Goes the Weasel!

Have you ever heard a woman speak who had a voice that was so sexy that you wanted to fuck her voice? I mean, if her voice had a vagina, I would fuck it! Wait - her voice *does* have a vagina!

My cat and I take turns using the toilet. He likes to pee and I like to drink. No... I have that backwards. *I* like to drink, and *he* likes to pee!

Human meat will someday become a commodity. Human meat marinades and rubs will become a common product. A whole new meaning will become associated with, "You rub me the wrong way."

If I had been born female, I still would have spent my life falling in love with girls. It just would have been *a lot easier to get laid*.

When I graduated high school, one girl said that I would go far in life. Thirty years later, I had gone far in life... Then I came back.

Did you know that a man can *always* see through a woman's skirt or dress if he really wants to? As the saying goes, hiney sight is always 20/20.

NEVER try to mow drunk! There can be serious consequences for you, the lawn, and sometimes even the lawnmower! In fact, there are *a lot* of kinds of technology that you should not attempt to operate while drunk!

I hate the airline corporations. I do understand that they have to sometimes cancel a person's flight; I just hate it when they do it *in flight*!

Chapter 5: Longer Jokes

The other day, I saw something on the carpet that I did not recognize. In fact, I was pretty sure I had never seen anything like it! I was completely confounded trying to figure it out, until I went over to pick it up. Suddenly, I realized what it was and why I didn't recognize it: It was a clean spot.

Someone asked me if I was in touch with my "inner woman"… Well, we used to text each other, and then she sent me a couple of pictures in the email. Eventually, we fell in love and got married. We now have two kids with another on the way.

Dicks are hungry. They will fuck any mouth, asshole, or pussy that they can get themselves inside of. Pussies, on the other hand, don't hunger for anything. They don't like dick, and they don't like pussy or titties. The only thing that pussies like is kids. When an asshole takes a crap, the result is shit; when a pussy takes a crap, it's a kid.

I plan to develop and market digital systems that will restore the rights of the average American slave. This is because I can program a computer better than I can program a politician. I leave the programming of politicians in the hands of the billionaires!

If you are dealing with a confrontation that might very well end in physical violence, it is better to use the nastiest rural accent that you can muster. If you are articulate and eloquent, you just *sound* like someone who is going to get his *ass kicked* by someone with bad rural grammar!

I was once dumped by a girlfriend after five days for Yort, of all people! I think it was because I was going back to college, and he was right there in town. Also, he had a bigger dick than me. He was right in town with a bigger dick, and not only was my dick smaller, but it was 800 miles away. From that distance… it looks REALLY small!

This woman who was a complete stranger asked me to fuck her in the bathroom of the Wal Mart; when she saw my penis she exclaimed, "You plan to fuck me with *that*?" I knew that it was not much, but it was the best I could muster under the circumcision.

You can't flip off the blind. Also, you can't yell insults at a deaf person. That is why when you are *really* mad at someone you have to both yell insults *and* flip them off, just in case they are lacking one of their primary senses!

Chapter 6: Bizarre Jokes and Simple Weirdness

I bet somewhere in history, it has been normal for a woman to lick her baby's butt clean. If you are a mammal, it is *normal* to lick assholes; if another mammal won't do it, then you lick your own.

Adieu and Adair and a doodie derriere…

"Peace and Quiet" or "Queafs in Private"?

Yup - Kiera Knightly shit in my mouth, but she is so skinny that it was actually *sexy!*

Jai Guru - Fuck You!

Child 1: "iPad"
Child 2: "iPod"
Child 3: "I peed."

I mean, as long as the sheep is really in *love* with you, and she wants to make love rather than just *fucking*, then it is okay. If you sincerely care about her, then it can still be a meaningful spiritually bonding experience.

In 2014, Phil didn't make a prediction because he was vaporized by a solar flare!

If you want a girlfriend who is *really* young, you have to ABORT her before you FUCK her!

I adore women; I think that they are *so* cute! If I had a dick, I would fuck every vagina on the planet!

Never suffer a *VEGAN* to live!

Wouldn't it be embarrassing if you were to emerge from a public john with just a little shit and toilet paper clinging to the corner of your mouth?

Some people just prefer their pussy dead before they fuck it…

If a slut enjoys a good gang-bang, she can become pregnant with fraternal triplets, each from a different father - a horse, a dog, and an ape!

I am an eater of other people's pussies.

I am *ALWAYS* coming across time for Sarah Connor...

Did you know that if you acquire enough money, you actually *become* Satan?

The guy with the cowboy hat always beats the *crap* out of the guy wearing a beanie.

Not being drunk today is getting *really old*!

I smell totally sweet to flies.

Strange *is* the new normal.

Have you ever messed up a relationship with a chicken?

I have underwear that has actually been condemned.

The thought of making a joke about circumcision is something that I have played around with a lot in my life.

Has there ever been a *human meat* connoisseur? Maybe the Aztecs?

Get the hell out of there! The irony is at a dangerous level!

There is just something about wearing women's "peanut butter"…

Just because someone is *fucking* you don't mean that they *like* you. Like corporations.

These days, "Angry" counts as a sexual orientation.

Authoritarians are people who have failed to get enough psychotherapy!

I never did get women figured out in life; I can barely figure out a cat!

If you do eat meat, there is no reason why you should not eat humans.

She didn't seem to really like me, but her *butt* sure did!

I named my kids after security cameras…

That's the whole thing about dying: you don't get anymore birthday parties, and you don't get to turn a year older.

First he was floating, and then he was sinking. Now he's rotting, although he's still breathing… I think he has Fish Leprosy!

When people ask me how old I am, I tell them that I am "forty-fuck". That's an actual age, isn't it?

Daylight Savings - how would that have worked in ancient times? How the fuck does one reset a sun dial?

Oprah Winfrey's SHIT is worth more on eBay than I am in real life!

"The water's broken…"
"Do you mean the plumbing?"
"No - the *water itself!*"

You know what they say, you can't MAKE
an omelet! *Only God can make an omelet!*

Monotheism was created to destroy Man's
covenant with God.

I have never left a bar with anyone who I
didn't *come* with.

A human is like a bucket; it's no good if
there is a hole in the bottom of it.

My intuition tells me that I need to shit; I
can just *feel* it in my gut!

People are the most evil people you will
ever meet.

I don't have a cock. *It* has a *man.*

They might play a few good tunes these
days, but POLITICS NEVER WILL!

Bestiality? I just say that where I lay my cat
is home.

It is rude to leave shit in a toilet that
someone else wants to drink out of....

I *almost* had some pussy, but I overthunk it!

If a woman is a lesbian, does that mean that she is both gay and angry at the same time?

My mother is better at negative spin than anyone I know.

I am a celibate omnisexual, and an anorexic omnivore.

Why don't they have a name for someone who is your spouse, but is either androgynous or a hermaphrodite?

I think that it is unforgivable the way that after 911, *all* terrorists were ostracized. I mean, socially, it is so un-cool.

People who become comics at a young age are lucky because they don't have to deteriorate into one as they get older!

For a while, a Microsoft program started performing correctly; it was *really* weird!

No, I didn't say that I crapped in my pants. What I said was that I *found* crap in my pants, but I didn't put it there. I suspect foul play…

I take women literally. A gal told me that I am a piece of shit, and I actually tried to flush myself down a toilet!

If you pick a woman up for a date, the first thing you should do is apologize for having a dick. For some reason, having a penis comes off as being *rude* to women.

Ever hear of "Horatio"? Well, your whore-ratio is the number of cunts to the number of dicks in a room.

Have you ever seen pure optimism expressed by a rooster?

Have you ever had someone commit suicide on your *first date?*

Dude: "Man, I'm pooped!"
Buddy: "Exhausted? Me too."
Dude: "No, I meant that I am carrying a load…"

Have you ever woken up and not really remembered what you had for dinner, then gone to your refrigerator and seen that the level of everything in there had gone down a little bit…

Why do they call the USA a "cuntry" when it is IMPOSSIBLE to get laid? A country with no cunt is like a winery with no wine!

I get really jealous when I find one of my own blonde hairs lying around the house…

Can anyone tell me what the mouse population of Mexico is?

There's this girl; I like her butt and her cunt.

"Overly-Estrogenated" - When you have so many female whore-moans raging through your system that you can't *help* but to be a cunt to everyone around you!

I live in a trailer so small that I have to store my dishes in the fridge.

A food scientist is known as a *cusinologist.*

<Said in a heavy rural accent :> You can't trust people these days - I always said!

No. I don't trust my clothing either; that's why I am not wearing it right now.

Theorem: As technology evolves, people become MORE DICKS!

Whenever a Sicilian baby is born, the FBI takes a picture of it for their records.

I *like* the freezer. It's one of my favorite places!

Advertising to innocent victims is totally unacceptable.

I am not just hungry; I am *angry* hungry. Basically, I am going to kill or eat anything that gets near me!

My floors are *way* too dirty to accommodate the five-second rule!

My wife is six years old... I got her on realdoll.com.

Have you ever kissed someone after giving her a Dirty Sanchez?

Date? Hell! At this point, I would be happy with date rape!

You know that you really are pathetic when you are actually grateful to have a stalker!

I have no way of *not* ranting against the billionaires.

It is better to have NO relationship with yourself than to have a *bad* relationship with yourself!

When a pedophiliac finds a baby in a dumpster, he calls it a matter of "Seren-Dip-Itty-Bitty".

Watching someone go senile is watching a loved one become stupider over time.

Now I know what it's like to be God - I can give life, but I can't have it myself.

I want to kick Sarah Palin in her prosthetic balls!

Fuck you! *You* fucked *me!* Go ahead and wash your own fuckin' dick!

I *still* don't know what *appropriate* audiences are. I have never met an audience that was appropriate in any way!

I have cats who won't even *try* to clean their asses, because they know that if they don't do it, I will…

Why is it that if you try to screw your girlfriend in the ass, instead of treating you like a friend she treats you like an enema?

Have you ever gone down on someone's ass, and come up with something in your mouth?

Everyone in the world has to be a dick in one way or another. Otherwise, we would just be a bunch of dickless assholes!

Never scratch your butthole and then pick your nose in that order…

Never kiss a shedding cat when your face is sweaty!

So I am a *dick*! But there's no point in dwelling upon the past…

Well FUCK ME! I know that I did.

Stick this on your thinking cap: Christianity is a form of insanity.

My cat tried to bury my shorts… after giving them a good sniff!

I love kids. They make such a satisfying crunch when you hit them with a mace!

If you pull your dick out of your wife's ass, and there is a turd on it, then you should spin her around, and shove it straight into her mouth.

If a woman is orally clam diving, does she sometimes find a pearl with her tongue?

I wish that my defecations were more fruitful…

One can never be surgically altered enough to be forgiven by a lesbian for having been born with a penis…

Ancient Proverb: You can always lie to the stupid.

Old Saying: 'Tis said a Klingon can slay a foe with butt a single fart!

Do you ever get the feeling you're being followed by a chicken?

"I have one full load of laundry."
"Just one load? That's not so bad."
"No. I mean that there is a *full load* in each of my shorts!"

Weird concept: "Pizza Flavored Bong Water"

I am a casserole architect.

Keep your friends close and your enemas even closer!

The other day I was talking to myself and I said, "Do you know what I mean?"

I don't know where my cat is. I'm not my brother's keeper.

I dunno'; cats are pretty crazy… I would hate to see one *actually* go psychotic!

Women think that men are totally fucked up. Of course they are right. But if women think that it is such a trip in the park, try *having a dick attached to your body!*

I have heard of a hobgoblin. What the heck is a-knob-goblin'?

Bitches? Are you *kidding me?* When it comes to bitches my *name is "DENIED"!*

In the end, every man will have some woman hurting him; she might as well be pretty.

I am out of booze. My cat wants in. My asshole feels "creamy". I think *I have* to go in!

Why is it that when my dick is small, it is the only part of my body that looks old?

I have wished for scissors when I have a pair in my pocket!

I have never met a female who knows how to retract her claws.

It had better be! If that cat is NOT purring, I am going to FUCKING KILL it!

I have no acquaintance with tits or pussy. I never get any further than the neck or the wrist.

I am happy to eat a woman's asshole; I just don't want her to poop in my mouth. I mean, a guy has to draw the line somewhere, right?

Redneck (spoken with a heavy rural accent): "People 'round here don't take *kindly* to people who take things *wrong*."

I just totally misread a cat!

If you sit in cat litter with sweaty balls, your nuts get frosted as though you had rolled a cookie in powdered sugar.

Treason is EXACTLY what billionaires do best!

I hate it when I am sitting on the john, and I just can't shit, but every time I go to wipe, a little more comes out...

Nice movie. They were "beating around the bush" the hole movie, then they did the unicorn reference at the end...

If a white unicorn represents a penis, then a black lion represents a vagina.

Friends are much more dangerous than enemies. Never trust anyone who is close to you.

If you trust a human, it is in the PERFECT position to hurt you!

Murdering a "Right to Lifer" is retro-active abortion.

What kind of fountain spurts "cock-candy"?

Being gestated is like being in prison for 9 months of every lifetime.

I thought it was over, and then my ass got a second wind...

Like Velcro on your nut-sack...

Have you ever tucked your dick back and gotten shit on the head of your cock?

Just the WORD "cummerbund" is enough for a Mexican to kick the crap out of your ass!

I don't hate Jews; I just think that *my* family doesn't deserve to survive!

It turns out that the Confederated States of America actually *won* the Civil War. It just didn't happen until the year 2000!

I hear that terrorists support gay marriage.

A friend asked me, "Do you want to go with us to a Beast Row?" I said, "I live on a farm… (Paws…) I'll guess I'll *come*, but only if I can *enter through the back door*."

Have you ever thought that you crapped your pants, then after checking it out, realized that you *only* farted?

I can *always* feel a cunt, even if it is in digital format!

When you get zits over night it is called "Sleep acnea".

Cats are like old people; they like to take a nap in the afternoon.

Most prosperous nation ever? Then why is it that most Americans can't *afford* to live in the USA?

I once realized that all of my children are reincarnations of …   each other.

I am so amazing and awesome that I only really have time to worship myself!

If you can think with your dick, can it write a joke?

I am not just a pussy hound; I like to think of myself as a pussy engineer!

Congratulations dear, we have a son! Excellent; I needed someone to beat up!

No, there isn't a woman hiding inside me; her penis wasn't long enough!

Do you ever taste your own shit on the dick you are sucking?

Have you ever actually met a woman who wanted to have sex? I haven't.

How to ruin any wedding: Just shove your hands into your pants and shit into your hands, then throw shit in every direction.

Well, *somebody's* gonna' get fucked, and I HOPE IT'S MY SEX DOLL!

They say that if you drink apple juice, your sperm tastes better. What if you eat chili powder and cumin? What does your sperm taste like then? Having cumin cum in your mouth is like having to smell a salami fart!

Never make an enemy of your body. It is in the perfect position to hurt you!

No study has ever been done that yielded results that prove conclusively that a Vegan is a human being.

Question: How frequently do you cook? If you said "frequently", then you answered the question. Don't be so easily manipulated!

Did you say nitro glycerin stories, or nitro glycerin suppositories?

I can't wait until yesterday.

Being turned down by an insurance company is like being rejected for a date by a whore.

Have you ever met a two year old baby crack whore?

Is it Microsoft Word, or "Microsoft?" - "Word!"

My sister is a baker trying to get her kids off gluten…

Did you hear about the genetic engineer who didn't believe in evolution?

Playing video games doesn't burn calories, but I am pretty sure that it does *create* them!

I didn't shit, and I didn't *not* shit. I came in here to piss, and there was some sort of anal activity involved!

Yea, it is a rat, but it works in a lab. It is fancy too, and works very hard. I call it an elaborate lab rat labor rat.

I fuckin' LOVE women! They have cunts *and* assholes; who's not going to love *that?*

I *think* I am going to fart. I am *definitely* going to fart... I am *glad* that it was *just* a fart!

This is the difference between a boy and a man: A boy mostly thinks about his own feelings, where a *man* on the other hand also thinks mostly about the boy's feelings...

This chick is *so* hot that my dick is way bigger than normal when hard; if I were to touch my dick right now, *I* would feel gay!

The mirrors in my house are all covered with sperm…

I once belched so hard that I threw my back out!

Oral sex is exclusive to mammals. Have you ever heard of a bird engaging in oral sex?

What would it be like? Hey baby, give me some beak!

Jack Sprat was super fat. His wife could eat no lean, and so between the two of them, they ate the dog.

It *not* that I am a fecalphiliac, it's just that if you love someone enough, it doesn't really bother you…

Think it's a hassle cleaning cat fur off the floor and furniture? Just try cleaning off of THE CAT!

This is actually true: there's a guy named "Kneel Bush"; sounds like cunnilingus to me!

I met this dude named Peter Dick Handcock; he was a real jerk-off.

My wife once told me that she had shaved her pussy for me. If that was true, then why was I shoving my face into a razor-sharp white Brillo pad?

The LONLIEST part of my lifetime, was my LIFETIME!

It would be great to be able to have a date without downloading an update….

I was trying to flirt with this gorgeous woman in the store the other day, so I told her that I was going to go home and dress my love doll up to look just like her!

If you do your brewing yesterday, then you can drink your brew today.

Being in my cat's arms is the safest place I know of.

Billionaires eat baby meat.

When they talk about "Television programming" they don't mean the shows you are watching; it is *you* who is being programmed.

God provides medicine, not Pfizer!

I AM NOT DRUNK! I am simply in a state of mildly sedated alcoholism.

It makes my *asshole hurt* just *thinking* about how beautiful Katrina Bowden is!

My dad had a lot of girlfriends, and it was never clear exactly which one was my mother...

I like women as a hole...

When you squeeze a woman's ass, you should put your fingers on the outside of her butt cheek, so that you can push your thumb into her asshole.

Are kitties smart? I have a cat who can do multiplication.

Why is it that you can't fart out of your dick?

Sorry I am getting back from lunch late, boss. It was a hummer nobber nooner.

It's fun to get a bitch drunk, so it takes a lot of the fun out of it if she is just drunk *all of the time*.

Duke: "Is there a cat abuse department to which I can submit a claim if I feel as though I am not receiving the treats that I want?"

If I actually touch a button on the computer, will it explode?

I am a Geriatriphiliac - I like to fuck old people, but only ones who are my slaves.

Cats, chickens and bees are a far cry from actual companionship.

It is better to realize that you have diarrhea than it is to crap yourself.

Well… she's old enough that she *could* have a bush, like, just *barely,* but, she has it waxed anyway…

I am NOT an anti-Semitist; it's just that I *am* Jewish…

Do you know what it is like to be a parent and a jungle gym at the same time?

Incest? What the fuck do you mean? I actually *resent* you for how unpleasant it was to fuck you in my dream!

If we were to exterminate them, I think that their lives would be better.

I didn't want to get my girlfriend pregnant, so I pulled out and blew my load all over her teddy bear's face.

Two young people in bliss… I had college and my future. She had her vagina….

If you are Sicilian, are you automatically *born* in a rage?

A LOT of women who are not lesbians eat pussy; pussy is one of the best things on Earth to eat!

My greatest asset in life is that I'm insane.

Humans are too stupid to bee trustworthy.

Being constipated is a long wait for a shit that don't come, where waiting for a woman to give up pussy is a long wait for a ship that don't come!

In combat this dude's guts got all slashed up in an episode of BladderScar ButtCracktica.

Rotting corpses and shit is bad environment in which to raise a child.

I was a half-breach entangled birth. I have never come out of or come into anything normally in my life!

If you are a girl, take this advice: ALWAYS wear a skirt, butt NEVER wear panties; a woman should be prepared to be fucked at all times!

Some people just feel better about being alive and being in their bodies if they are brainwashed. So pick a religion, and go to church.

You can create a universe within another universe; it's just that most people don't do it.

Men think that women with long necks are good at deep throat.

I wouldn't be a gentleman if I didn't try to fuck you in your cunt, mouth, AND asshole!

Your turd on my cock is no skin off my back.

It's not always that people commit suicide so much as that sometimes they just get tired of hanging out with themselves.

My son might be muddy, but at least he's COMPREHENSIVE!

I threw a movie party and one of my friends brought a porno; I should have seen that one coming!

Is it even POSSIBLE to get a celibate woman pregnant?

At the age of 50, you have a great deal of confidence if you can fart without having to go to the bathroom to do it.

FUCK the hills! If I can even tell you that my BEES are alive, I'll be happy!

A young cunt goes from peach-fuzz to pussy hair that is soft and fluffy. My wife's on the other hand, was like gray Brillo.

Dicks are like rugs; sometimes you have to take it out and beat it for a while.

You KNOW it's dirty, when even your
vacuum needs dusting!

I'm not against Jews as a *concept*!

If you are obsessed with receiving felatio,
and never get any, it REALLY SUCKS!

I wanted to make the DVD on my TV play,
but I reached for the mouse...

How do you tie a horseshoe?

I never pay for ass until I have sniffed it first.
I'm "smell-a-butt".

Do you know how really old pictures and
movies are all in black and white? That is
because color had not been invented yet, and
everything REALLY WAS in black and
white!

Old people walk as though they have their
pants around their ankles, which is only
sometimes true.

"High Fructose Corn-a-Cola"

Is that appropriate? After all, it is the 90's...
or at least it *used* to be.

Can a plant die of a broken heart?

If chicks go to school, why is it that no one teaches them the word "yes"?

Jesus Christ always did have a taste for pussy…

Well, if it is *your* city, then it certainly is not mine! I am not going to *share* a city with anyone!

It is easier to wear a Dirty Sanchez when you have no sense of smell.

Do you turn your pillow over when there is cum all over it?

Can you get so old that you literally have chunks of lint on yourself at all times?

It's just polite to fuck a chick in her mouth first. That way, she doesn't have to taste her pussy or her own asshole…

Someone once asked me if I was kidding him. I told him, "I am a comedian. I never kid."

The LAST thing I want to think about when I am coming is my wife!

I was dating this super skinny fourteen year old girl, and I made her get a "Bolivian" so I could pretend that she was only five.

My wife was an angry red-headed Sicilian going through menopause!

There is NO WAY you are going to be able to push a giant boot through a pant leg. That would be like trying to push a human head through a vagina!

Have you ever smoked to the point where you can't remember whether you have taken a hit? Well if I spaced out and forgot to *take* a hit, then I must have been stoned enough anyway!

Man - a chick with an ass *that* nice; I want to fuck all of her holes, just to make sure that everything's covered!

Cheekbones are the butt-cheeks, and the mouth is the asshole of the face.

Right now in America, there are millions of people getting *fatter;* I can almost hear it happening!

Who do you think gets representation: the billionaire who bribes your senator, or the person who goes out and votes?

Anyone who lives with a cat knows what it is like to have pussy hair in his mouth.

This is NOT my cat's hair in my mouth; someone snuck into my room and put someone else's cat hair in my mouth as I slept!

I like to drink "Alco Hall Lick Beaver Ages". In the hall, I like to lick beaver for ages.

Providing a source of meat is the only thing that humans have ever done of worth in this universe.

There is this brunette chick on Haven that I really like, because her eyebrows make her look *really surprised* all of the time.

I was pretty pleased, with honey and sugar on it.

I hate that thing!
What thing?
*EVERY*THING!

I did NOT take the Lord's name in vain; I took the *other* Lord's name in vein.

Things are getting bad when you have to wash your cleaner.

My mother has *selective* senility; she remembers everything that my sister says, and nothing that I do!

Having a "gourmet" coffee is always a *dick in your mouth!*

This is not a joke; it is just advice: If you like buttered popcorn, buy some fresh garlic cloves at the store, and press or mince the garlic into a pan with melted salted butter. Simmer it for a couple of minutes to make a strong garlic butter and apply *that* to your popcorn. Your taste buds will thank you!

To start one episode of The Guild, I pointed my flashlight at the screen, and turned it on...

I know that I have to go to the bathroom, but that shit just ain't happening!

I have learned to listen to what I say, and I haven't learned so much my entire life!

She's 21? Old enough to drink - old enough to be eaten!

I think that when it comes to ass-fucking, proprieties must be observed!

The best thing about being your own sexual partner is that she is always in the mood, and you know for sure that she is never unfaithful!

Do you think that I should put on clean underwear JUST because it is Thanksgiving? ...Nah! That would be dumb!

My mother is getting quite senile. She has a brain, but it offends her to attempt to use it.

My rooster is seriously confused; he is always trying to get pussy from a chicken instead of a cat.

I adore women. In fact, I *respect* women tremendously! Well... if I respect women, I obviously haven't been laid in *six years or so!*

Do my fingers smell like *my cat's* asshole?

Believe me, making *me* feel like I am nothing is LIVING IN THE FUCKING PAST!

My Spelling and Grammar Checker software got so frustrated that it just gave up on me!

I measure atmospheric precipitation based on what I find on my living room floor!

There's just something about a gal getting gang-banged by a pack of dogs…

Well, if suicide isn't a very positive experience for you, then maybe you aren't doing it right!

George W. Bush has his fist stuffed so far up the ass of whoever is the current president that he can operate his mouth like a puppet!

It would kill me to go a week without pussy! Good thing I have 10 cats!

I built an oven that bakes buns, bread, and pizza, and it also fires ceramics! It's Hairy Pottery too!

I found myself standing in the kitchen eating a jar of tartar sauce. It must have been the munchies!

I knew this guy who was so sure of what he was, that he came out to his family and the entire community when he was 17. That's right; since he was a teenager he's been *openly* Jewish!

I do *not* hate white people for being evil. I have *lots* of reasons to hate white people; in addition to that, they just *happen* to be evil. ☺

To use the toilet, I sometimes have to wait in line… behind the cat.

Chapter 7: Weird Trips

If you are in the advertisement industry, Satan has one fist up your ass, and the other one up your cunt, and is controlling your brain and your mouth from there.

I have a fish who likes cats.

The happiest dogs have owners who are senile. They will get fed ten times a day if they can. They'll just shit a lot…

I once heard a man say that he didn't believe in evil. In fact Evil *does* exist; it bleeds crude oil and it ejaculates dollars and cents!

I have been broken up with a hundred times more often than I have even *had* a girlfriend! Chicks just look at me and they *can't wait* to break up with me. They just run up to me and reject me to save time!

I once knew a woman who taught her cat to lick pussy…

The thing about the medical industry is that they illustrate how Pfizer has their fist shoved up the ass of the American consumer!

If you are single, you might consider it normal to have a meal in front of the fridge consisting of nothing but condiments.

God is a dick; Christ is a dick. Do you *really* think that you are forgiven? Or that being forgiven would save you from *going to Hell*?

Cats can actually *taste* money; they always prefer the most expensive treats!

Japanese-made cellular phones can brainwash American values into other Asian cultures!

This chick let me stick my dick in her, and I knew that she was a girl, not a woman. I knew this because I know that women do not sleep with men. Women get together with other women. If you are a guy and like to insert you penis into vaginas, then I suggest that you look for girls who are too innocent to know (as women do) that pussy is *way* hotter than dick!

My cat will sniff something ONE TIME, and if he doesn't want to eat it, he will try to burry it! It is either food or shit; there is no in-between.

Goat flelching: I know that there are a huge number of men in the West and Midwest who stick their cocks in goats' assholes, cunts, and mouths. In fact, I have *never* met a farmer, redneck, or cowboy who didn't fuck at least one of his goats or, lacking goats, some other kind of livestock. My problem with this is that I am not willing to commit rape. If a goat is a nasty little girl, and she wants to take the hard one, then I am willing to FUCK her! On the other hand, if she wants to make out for a while, and kiss on the lips or even with tongues, then that is fine with me, and then we can make love, but the *consent* of the goat is required for me to have a good time.

It is important to distinguish my chickens as livestock, and not pets. Legally, if they are livestock, they belong to me and by extension their eggs are also my property. However, if they are considered pets, then I am their Guardian, and their eggs legally belong to them. Were that the case, I would be required to enter into an arrangement with them in order to obtain the eggs.

From the perspective of human culture, my land belongs to me. However, I think that from the perspective of the land, it is we who belong to it.

My cat dunked his ass into my drink. No one knows why.

I got some manure delivered and one of my chickens got on top of it and took a shit; I was so mad that I crapped on the chicken shit!

Have you ever stood up during an entire performance because you didn't want to miss the end, and you didn't want to sit down because you had shit your pants?

Pfizer wants me to think that women constantly obsess about getting a bigger cock. It's not like they have a life or any serious concerns; they just think about how nice it would be for someone to shove a telephone pole up their collective snatches.

The video interface went out on my digi camera, so now it can only take pictures of blackness…

Women can do amazing things with their minds. Men's strengths lie elsewhere.

Shitting and pissing can sometimes be a matter of self-expression. Like a puppy that pisses because he is so happy and excited that he can't contain himself. Dogs also sometimes crap as a way of saying "hello".

There is no explaining a chicken's logic. I actually saw a chicken walk *voluntarily* into an oven! The irony was intense, but the chicken was unaware of it. Chickens can be smart at times, but mathematics is a level of logic that escapes them.

I fucked a dog once. It wasn't because I was horny, nor was it because I thought that Max deserved to get raped. It was because of the context. I was at a political convention, and I did it for shock value!

Titgina: An artificial vagina that is also a breast augmentation. It allows a man to fuck a woman inside her tit. It fact, they could surgically enhance a woman to have a vagina anywhere she does not already have one, just so that she could get the gang bang of a lifetime!

My dad liked to tell the following joke: "Snake! Snake! Hit it with a baby!" I find it ironic that this came from a man who *actually* once used his 18 month old baby girl as a club!

You could take a white person, put them between two fuckin' slices of white bread, add mayonnaise, and throw on a cooked egg white! You would have not only a pretty good sandwich, but also the whitest fucking thing on the planet! Why don't you wrap it in a sheet of white paper?

We are human, and we have to eat to live. That is the way of the world. That is, unless you have that ancient Vedic technique that allows you to go months at a time without eating at all… However, back *then,* they were not doing it to lose weight!

If you don't want a woman to attack you and eat you, then try to not *smell* like her prey. I mean, if you were going to feed some lions in the zoo, you wouldn't rub yourself in bloody steaks before entering their cage, right? Like that.

Life Insurance must be the biggest scam of all time; it doesn't matter once you are dead, and you can't use it while you are alive! If you make a claim, they will raise your rates and deductible!

Drug sluts are awesome! You put drugs in one end, and then you can shove your dick in the other. Of course, this has never worked for me. If I had only been born ugly and stupid, I would probably have at least one wife and lots of kids by now!

These days, there are a lot of different kinds of sexuality. Omni-sexuality, my personal favorite, requires a person to be vegesexual, minerasexual, and animasexual simultaneously. People also commonly ignore mineraphilia, vegephilia, and bestiality. If you have sex with humans, then you have sex with animals. Can a person be bacteriasexual? Or fungisexual?

I have heard that you can't be a beggar AND a chooser, but my sister proved to me that one CAN be a choosey little beggar!

Reverse psychology always works. The fastest way to get someone to *not* visit you is to give them an open invitation to visit any time they want. I told my mother and sister that my farm was open to visitors and tours for the entire year. I have never had *nobody* come out to visit so much ever before!

You know who should qualify for Medicinal Marijuana? Fat people! I don't know why but when I see a fat person (and in Iowa, I see a LOT of them!), I always think that someone should get them stoned right away! They just sort of look sick to me…

This FedEx dude was actually trying to use his brain. It was sad, but at the same time it was almost cute, for a human!

Have you ever noticed that everything that is German is meaner than the same equivalent in other cultures? For instance, a German Shepherds are one of the meanest dogs ever, and German Nazis are some of the meanest people ever. It's true of German bees too.

The Italian bees just want to ferment some honey and have a big bee orgy. German bees are all like, "Hey! Fuck you!" and then they sting your ass!

I know that this sounds dumb, because water is not alive, but what if they could genetically engineer water? Would it be like the GE cabbage, eggplant, and tomatoes? Those commercial produce have appearance, but no substance, not even flavor. Would they be able to produce water that will not quench your thirst?

I don't give a fuck about your low fat ice cream and low fat whipped cream; I don't give a crap about your low sodium chocolate syrup or your low carb cherries! If you want to lose some weight, then put down the *fucking sundae fat-ass*!

If you think that it is hard to have a long-distance relationship with a virtuous woman, just try having one with a *slut!* She might be faithful to you for a couple of days, but as soon as you are away, your best friend gets released from prison and it's *ALL OVER!*

Chinese culture can be traced back six thousand years. There are Christians who think that the world is only four thousand years old, even though we know that civilization goes back at least ten thousand years. So what does that make the Chinese, Gods? (And what does that make God, Chinese?)

I once saw my cat sneak into the chicken's coup and eat some Layer Crumbles, which is very odd behavior for a cat. I don't think that he does it anymore. He was probably put off the first time he found a fresh turd in the bowl.

Do know what I call Pro-Choicers? I call them baby murderers! I can tell you now that I *despise* anyone who is not into baby murder! Do you know what I have to say to the Pro-Lifers? FUCK YOU! If they are my kids, I will murder them if I want to!

Forcing sexual orientation upon someone who is celibate is like accusing an atheist of being affiliated with a religion.

I don't give a crap about what people think about me. I don't give a crap about anything in the world. I even kicked my dog in the balls the day after I had him castrated.

Jesus Christ was the first true celebrity and comedian. They say that Jesus was celibate? Bullshit! Jesus would fuck *anyone!* A drunken Jesus fucking a goat and saying, "It's all about *love!*"

If you can't get laid, then at least you can make jokes about the fact that you can't get laid, and if you can make gals laugh, then *maybe* you can get laid! The problem with this joke is that if you tell it, you will *never* get laid!

If you were a girl whose puberty was brought on by smoking pot at the age of nine, then you are a "Mari-woman".

God's Major Mistake: "I really regret this one thing. ☹ I gave them CHOICE, and then they chose GREED! This is what is wrong with the billionaires and their corporations."

The *original* Darwin Award went to some prehistoric schmuck who tried to eat the berries from a poison ivy vine.

I brought this little girl kitten home, and she looked at me and decided that I have *some* intelligence, so I am worth educating…

First Class is always at the *front* of the plane, so among other perks; the First Class passengers are paying for the right to hit the ground first if the plane crashes.

Yup, my cat screwed up the system, but I made the mistake of trying to *fix the system* rather than realizing the situation I was in biologically… A lot of dudes have realized that they got someone pregnant for the same reason!

Chapter 8: Cruel Ironies

People don't like being friends with people who don't have friends. If you are new to an area, people can dislike you just because you don't know anybody.

If a chick rejects you, the next one is *twice* as likely to reject you. If the next gal rejects you, then the one after that is *four times* as likely to reject you. After that, the next one is eight times as likely to reject you, and the next one after that is sixteen times as likely to reject you. If a man is rejected too many times by women, then his chances of getting a date become *astronomical!*

Most women are turned off sexually by the smell of shit. That is why it is good to take a shower before trying to seduce a woman. When a woman rejects a man, it causes something that women perceive to smell like shit to cover the man. That is why when a woman rejects you, the next one is more likely to reject you, and so on and so forth…

Some of the FEW times I have been laid have been in dreams, so I think it counts.

If you don't have a woman in your life, you not only have to live without pussy, but you also have to suffer the stigma of being gay. ☹ You end up with no wife and no kids, and everyone gets to hate you for your loneliness. Humans suck!

Chapter 9: Things that Piss Me Off!

Being Rejected

The things that women say when they are blowing you off is amazing. I am an expert at being blown off by women, and 90% of the time, they will claim to have a boyfriend whether it is true or not.

Chicks have told ME that I need a girlfriend AFTER denying me pussy! Seriously! I think that I am the ONE person who *knows* that I need a girlfriend, and that is why I was trying to get my dick in her pussy!

"You're *trying* too hard!" is another thing they say. I heard that one over and over again. "You're *trying* too hard!" "You're *trying* too hard! Maybe something would happen if you wouldn't try so hard!" How the hell can you try *less* hard when you are being denied pussy? The more I am rejected, the more desperate I will become, and I don't know how to try *less hard* at that point! I have been told to just, "Give it to God." Or "Give it to Nature and let that higher power resolve the situation. Nature abhors a vacuum." I tried that too. When I give the situation to a higher power, do you know what happens? *NOTHING!*

Here's another line chicks like to give you when they are blowing you off, "It will happen for you *some day."* Well guess what? It fucking *DIDN'T*! Chicks just say that to get you out of their faces, and don't really give a crap if it does or does not happen for you, "some day."

I heard many women tell me that, "I am on *Mother Devine."* Translated from TM Movment-eese, this is a way of saying that she is celibate. Curious how often I have heard that from a woman who ends up with kids and married to *someone else.*

I have also had women tell me, "I wouldn't want to hurt you." Well I say, freaking hurt me! What does she plan to do? Go find a man who is *more qualified* to be hurt?

I also hate it when you tell a gal that you love her, and she says, "Love me? You don't even *know* me!" I had just hoped that we could see if we would enjoy getting to know each other. In time, maybe we would fall in love with getting to know each other, and some day, we could pledge to spend the rest of our lives loving getting to know each other…

Stupid Iowans

Since moving to Iowa, Native Iowans have proven to be the most special source of mental retardation I have ever witnessed.

I used to work for Intermec Technologies Corporation in Cedar Rapids, Iowa. The administration occasionally required some sort of retarded meeting pertaining to carpal tunnel syndrome, or how to use Outlook (duh!), or sometimes an OSHA Safety Meeting. This seems harmless enough, until one is exposed to the information in the meeting. I once went to one of these *required* OSHA meetings, and one thing that the lecturer said was that "A very high voltage will kill you." I, of course, raised my hand and pointed out that he was wrong. A high *wattage* will kill you. Ever had a static electric shock? Those are thousands of volts at a very low current, and with a very brief exposure time. It is the voltage *times* the current that gives overall power, and it is the *power* that can cause harm, not the voltage alone. The guy admitted that he was wrong, and went on to the fire safety segment of the meeting. He said that the main cause of death in a fire was suffocation. BONG! Wrong again idiot! Any fireman or fire Marshall can tell you that the greatest danger is the respiration of toxic gases caused by burning of modern day building, architecture, and furniture materials. The *gases* inhaled by people in a burning structure cause far more deaths than people simply suffocating. I pointed this out to the OSHA guy too, but he refused to back down, and insisted that what he said was the official OSHA perspective. I think that he just didn't want to admit once again that he was a fucking retard who didn't understand the material on a scientific level *at all*. I dropped the issue, but in the context that he was giving a SAFETY lecture, his *wrong* information served to *endanger* the lives of the people in the meeting, not protects them.

Years before that I was in another very silly safety meeting, and the lecturer was talking about particles which are hazardous in the workplace. He listed several examples, and asked the audience to give more examples of kinds of particles in the workplace that could be hazardous. I volunteered, "Radiation." The guy next to me (a janitor) leaned over and mentioned quietly in a heavy rural accent, "Radiation isn't a particle; it's a ray." I didn't think that I should initiate a debate about it in the meeting, so I let it slide, but *HOTLY JUMPING MONKEY BALLS!* Being on the maintenance staff, I am assuming that this guy didn't get a very high degree in school. I, on the other hand, got a degree in Computer Science, and an "A" in Calculus, Probability, and Quantum Physics. I know very well that a sub-atomic particle is a discreet manifestation of a field of nature that is present at all times and in all places, and that it can been seen as either a wave or a particle, depending on conditions and perspective. A "Ray" on the other hand, is either an abstract mathematical construct, or an optical illusion caused by light being filtered in some places and not others, like sunshine beaming through a break in a cloud. This guy didn't know what he was talking about, and that a janitor thought that he could correct and engineer on a scientific matter is a crazy iron all by itself! Fuckin' Iowans man!

A few years back, I was sending off a Priority package a few days before Christmas. It was Airsoft BB's for an internet customer. Of course, when Christmas gets near, vendors make an additional effort to get products to the customer as quickly as possible. When I got to the top of the drive, I saw that I had missed the mail man, but knew that he would be coming past going the other way in a few minutes. When he came back, I flagged him down, and when he pulled over and opened the window, I handed him the package. He said, "Yippifya… yippifya… yippifya…" which mostly left me perplexed. Eventually he blurted out part of a sentence resembling English and said in a super heavy rural accent, "It'll help if yuh..." and then he gestured and pointed at the package, and then at the mailbox. Okay, I get it. He was telling me that I should have put it in the mailbox. God forbid that he should have been able to finish that sentence! And after all, after working for the post office for years, one can't expect that he might have learned the terms for "package", "parcel" or "mailbox", right? Further, there is no way he could have learned these words in school, because in Iowa, there is no education in the schools.

Similar to the OSHA meetings, Iowa required children to go to slave indoctrination centers where they are NOT educated in schools. They are lied to about whether George W. Bush was a president or the first illegal dictator of the USA. The "students" heads are filled with propaganda, brainwashing, and mental manipulation in order to turn them into retarded, complacent, consumer-slaves for the oil corporations. These kids drink soda infused with HFCP, which is actually distributed in automated machines in the schools! HFCP is well known to cause obesity, diabetes, and mental retardation, and the "kids" that this process is producing are fat, unmotivated, and nearly useless beyond being good slaves for the aristocracy. Iowa has no system of education. It has a system of Slave Training.

So, being the most retarded state in the union, one can't expect Iowan lawmakers to show any level of enlightenment, or intelligent thought processes. Since Iowans are already super stupid, I think that it is a terrible mistake to allow them to use non-hands free cellular technology while operating a motor vehicle. Of course it is illegal anyway, because there is also a law that says that one must have one's hands on the steering wheel at all times, unless operating integrated automobile equipment (like the turn signal.) However, Greg Francisco, FFPD, tells citizens, "It is not illegal to use a cellular phone while driving." How the hell do you expect people to NOT break the law, when the police are actually *advocating endangering the lives of innocent people*? Only a piece of shit would use a cell phone while driving anyway, but I think that using a hands-free solution is an adequate compromise. There might not be a law against using a cell phone while driving in Iowa Per Se, but it is unforgivable that the law enforcement community *encourages* people to break the law while acting in a dangerous and irresponsible manner! Iowan laws suck; Iowan cops suck!

When I moved out to my farm, I wanted a phone in the garage for my business. As an engineer, I thought it would be a simple matter to run a wire from the junction box to my garage, and bill it as a second line on the regular phone bill for my address. But NO! In Iowa, they have to make *everything* into a complicated and retarded procedure! When I asked the phone company to come out and run phone lines to the garage and my new trailer, they told me that it could not be done. I was told that in order to have phones in additional buildings, that those buildings would also have to have street addresses of their own. This made no sense to me. If I want another phone in the chicken shed, I'll just run a wire. I don't think that the freaking chickens need a street address! The phone company told me to call them back after I have had street addresses assigned to the building in need of phones. So, I called the post office thinking that it would be a simple matter for them to assign a couple extra street addresses, one for my residence, and one for my business in the garage. BUT NO! The post office told me that the correct procedure was to contact the Sheriff and have him send out a man with a GPS unit, who would then assign the new addresses. The deputy did come out, and eventually I was able to get my phone lines. Now let's go over this again, in order to simply get a phone hook up in my garage, I ended up having to deal with three different organizations, and eventually have the Sheriff's department send out a deputy JUST TO GET A FUCKING PHONE LINE! Jesus fucking Christ, what the fuck do you think you people are doing!?? And after that, would you even expect them to handle your service in a non-retarded manner? No, I guess not. After living here eight years, the phone company has *NEVER* gotten my phone number OR address right in the phone book! They list my personal phone with my name, but they list my *business* phone number! Further, the address listed is on the North side of the street! All of my addresses are even numbers, and the one in the phone book is an odd number! What retarded dicks! After eight years, they *still* have it wrong. Well, the glass is half full. If I see someone come a shoot my neighbor, I will know to run and hide!

Bandito

Does anyone remember the Frito Bandito? He was a character used in Fritos advertisements in the 1970's and 1980's. They got rid of him because he was considered *politically incorrect* towards Mexicans! So what's up with the Pillsbury Doughboy? Doesn't he display a politically incorrect attitude towards Midwestern American Caucasians?

Dicks who only THINK they are Cooks

You know what pisses me off? People who put recipes on AllRecipes.com that are *not* recipes; like the baby back ribs marinade recipe that just calls for commercially purchased BBQ sauce. Mixing two cans of Campbell's Soup together and calling that a recipe is another example. Bullshit I say! You want to cook, start with raw and fresh ingredients. Grow as much of it yourself as you can, and get the most natural of what you can't grow. Mixing other companies' pre-made foods is NOT a recipe, it is simply food *assembly*. If you want to enjoy using a kitchen and create the most amazing food, then learn to make everything from scratch. Even grind you own gains by hand. Never buy from a retail outlet or a corporation any time that it can be avoided!

GPS

If you own a GPS unit, you are a dick. Big Brother is watching you at all times. The demographics data alone is worth billions to them annually. I plan to go into more detail on this subject in my next book.

Technology is Dangerous

I used to think that anything new was automatically cool. After being an engineer for years, I no longer believe this. I do sometimes long for the days when the internet was new and not so commercialized. Gaming was innocent, and the future of technology seemed bright. Now, technology is used to distract retarded people from the deterioration of our culture. Kids no longer care to learn or even play, except for video games. Video games used to be an innocent distraction from studying and extra curricular activities, but it has now become an obsession. Being social used to be restricted to dances and parties, but now it is a distraction from classroom time, and the young are divided between actual reality and virtual reality at all times. New computer games and technology used to be exciting, now it has become a "Dark Ages" of slavery and the destruction of human intelligence. I am not saying that a person should not use the internet, or play some games; I am just saying to not leave actual reality behind entirely. Spend some time doing something outside every day. Do something productive every day (and I literally mean, create something, a product or service.) Learn to be able to live without the support of society. Don't allow yourself to be turned into a retarded, complacent consumer-slave.

Not a real Political Spectrum

It behooves the aristocracy to keep the slave class fighting within themselves. We are presented with a political spectrum that is one dimensional. It is represented as a line, and you are either on the left, in the middle, or on the right. This in no way represents the reality of politics. A political struggle is by definition the rich vs. the poor, not the right against the left. "Liberal" in the context of politics is supposed to mean the Liberal use of government vs. the Conservative use of government. This defies the way we normally think about it. By definition, the Conservative element is supposed to believe that the power should be in the hands of the individual and private interests (Corporations), and the Liberals are supposed to advocate power lying mostly in the hands of the government. In our society, the "Liberals" seem to be the poor masses, and the "Conservatives" seem to support the government trampling upon the slave class. It is exactly the opposite of the definition of the terms. My scheme for a political spectrum is two dimensional, and incorporates up and down as well as left and right. The top represents the aristocracy, and the bottom represents the slave class. If you are near the top of the spectrum, then you support the aristocracy and their power over society. If you are near the bottom, then you believe in rights and liberty for the slave class of the culture. In the USA, they also spin "left" vs. "right" as liberal morals compared to conservative morals. That is also bullshit. As usual, the aristocracy is just trying to confuse the slave class by presenting them with non-political issues to argue about, while their rights are being destroyed. The cruel irony here is that the aristocracy, through greed, bribes, and lobbying, gets 100% of the representation in the government, the government *they* stole, while paying no tax at all, due to loopholes for the rich. At the same time, the slave class in America pays 100% of the taxes, and gets no representation at all!

Chapter 10: Bits

The Man VS the Dude

You all know who the Man is right? The Man restricts your freedom, and puts you in handcuffs, right? The Dude, on the other hand, is the friend of the little guy. The Man tracks you all of the time using the GPS in your cell phone. The Dude avoids GPS technology all the time, at all costs. The Man tells you that you can't have medicinal marijuana; the Dude always has a joint for you. The Man bribes senators; the Dude realizes that all politics are corrupt. The Man wants to sell you garbage dressed up to look like healthy, natural, organic food; the Dude has a greenhouse, and can cook you the most delicious meal possible out of actual healthy home grown food. The Man sells manufactured foods in a retail store; the Dude raises animal and vegetable nutrition from scratch on a farm. The Man lies all the time, through the News, advertising, and misleading packaging; the Dude always tells it like it is. The Man wants you to have two or more GPS devices on you at all times; the Dude doesn't even own a phone. The Man destroys justice, democracy, and your rights; the Dude supports the rights of the slave class over the rights of the aristocracy!

Quantum Kitties

Kitty cats sometimes like to do things, or appear to do things that are magical.

One time I was being bothered by a room mate's cat while I was trying to do homework. I put her out but she never actually seemed to be out. I took the kitty to the back yard, and closed the porch door. I looked out the window and verified that the cat was sitting right there in the back yard. I then went into the house and closed and locked the door from the hall to the porch. I turned around and was so surprised to see the cat sitting right there in the middle of the kitchen floor that I actually jumped in the air and screamed!

I was talking to my mom on the phone one winter day and was watching outside where some birds were feeding. I was looking straight at one bird one second, and in less than a second there was a blur of light, what appeared to be a gray smudge on the real-estate of my visual landscape, and in less than a second I was looking right at a cat sitting there with a bird in its mouth! Did the kitty move more quickly than my visual perception and cerebral cortex could process, or did the kitty actually *surpass the speed of light?*

Krishna and the Shepherdess

When I was at Maharishi International University, I heard an ancient Indian legend in which the Lord Krishna made love to six thousand shepherdesses all at the same time. I found myself wondering how he accomplished such a feat. Sure, he was a God, but what are the actual mechanics of such an act? I finally concluded that he used *consciousness!* He reached out to the clitoris of every one of the shepherdesses with his mind and vibrated them just like I was buzzing my embouchure on a woman's clit!

Pussy Buzzing

Now this is a technique which is much easier to accomplish if you have already played some sort of bilabial aerophone, that is, a brass instrument (or a didgeridoo.) I saw a comic act in which the comedian described how to make a whirring noise using you lips and vocal cords, and said that it can give a woman a very powerful orgasm. I thought, well, if a vibrator feels so good to a woman, why not apply what I learned about playing the trumpet? I can buzz into a mouthpiece without having the trumpet attached. I can also buzz my lips without even using a mouthpiece. I can also play many tunes on my lips, including the Star

Spangled Banner and Happy Birthday. I
even take requests! I would like to see a
vibrating dildo pull *that* off!

Fart Connoisseur

Have you ever heard off egg-farts? My sister
used to have them when we were young.
She liked to fart in my face, because I was
so much smaller, and it seemed to me that
the scent of her fart was similar to the food
she had been eating a few hours earlier. Can
we conclude that to someone who has a very
refined sense of smell, like a dog, your farts
might smell like bratwurst on one occasion,
deviled eggs on another, and asparagus on
yet another occasion? If so then answer me
this one question: what do my farts smell
like after I have been eating pussy?

The Nature of Humans

Your mind is your enemy. Why do I get
the impulse to stab myself in the face with a
knife? Why do I get the impulse to pee on
strangers? Do parents actually for an instant
think about throttling their child to death?
Do you ever pick up a knife and have some
deep thought about stabbing anyone who is
near you? If you are petting a dog or cat, do
you ever get an impulse to strangle them for
no reason? I think that people have all kinds
of bizarre impulses, and that the only thing

that distinguishes someone who can live peacefully in society and the psycho who is in an institution, is that some people have the self-control to master their behavior, and others just go around doing whatthefuckever pops into their heads!

Pig Mentality

My dad had the most unusual attitude toward food. He was an excellent cook, and pulled off such culinary acrobatics as de-boning a pheasant from the inside, de-boning two chickens and stuffing one bird with the other one, and roasting up a suckling pig for Christmas one year! He also used to eat raw sausage as he mixed it up, eat large squares of butter as though they were fudge, and drank directly from the corn oil bottle as though it was an energy drink! He not only ate large amounts of food, but at dinner he would eat with a serving spoon filled to overflowing, just so he could stuff the food into his face as quickly as possible. He ate so voraciously that his jaw would pop. He was a glutton, and weighed up to 360 pounds! He would eat or at least try basically anything considered food, and truly had the mentality of a pig! After Christmas dinner, I saw him break open the skull of the pig, and eat its brain! I wonder if that had something to do with it...

Sex Doll

You can now go to realdoll.com and buy
yourself a surrogate woman made out of
silicone over a metal chassis. This is a very
nice thing to have if women won't sleep
with you. I think that most men live and die
as virgins, because women can't stand to
touch a penis. Also, just keeping your love
doll in the bedroom to fuck occasionally is
not nearly as interesting as if you role-play
the situation a bit. Keep her in your living
room or kitchen, and interact with her
verbally and socially. Say high to her in the
morning, and kiss her goodnight when you
go to sleep. When you do make love to her,
so do under a low light, such as a couple of
candles. The low light softens her curves,
and makes her appear more like a real
woman from up close. Making love to a
silicone woman is not the same (or as good)
as making love to a living woman, butt it is
a hole lot better than jacking off all the time!

Pen and Sword

They say that the pen is mightier than the
sword. If the pen is so freaking powerful,
then the internet is really the bomb!

Dude, if your pen is mightier than your
sword, you should get your sword sharpened.

People are going to laugh at you if you walk onto a battle field and your main weapon is a pen. What are you going to do? Point it at targets and yell "Pow!"? Write down, "Bang!" on a piece of paper and hold it up for the enemy to see?

It is all based on context. If I am about to chop your head off with my sword, you had better hope to fucking God that you have a gun and not a pen in your hand!

My Dike Chicken

I have a chicken, a brown leghorn, who *hates* the rooster. She will stay inside all day, and won't go out until he comes in, in the evening. I think that he has jumped her a couple of times, as roosters will do, and she considered it rape. She hangs out all day with another hen named Marva. If the rooster comes in, she'll leave, and if he goes out, she will return to the hen house. That's right; I think that my chicken is a lesbian!

Chapter 11: Dream Stories

In addition to having a particularly deranged mind, it is not very surprising that I have had some very bizarre dreams in my life. I once dreamed about kissing Sandra Chalke down by the creek. I didn't even know I *liked* her before that!

Gwyneth Paltrow

A little while ago I dreamed that I was kissing Gwyneth Paltrow. This made me very happy, because I had had a crush on her for years! I made an internet shrine to her once. In the dream, I went to kiss her again, and she declined. She said that she was just being polite the first time. For some reason, she did want to be friends, and she and I went for a walk together. We were happy and playful, and it was sweet. Do you remember a game called "Devil on the Doorstep" when you were a kid? To play it, one knocks or rings at a person's door, then runs away. Well, Gwyneth liked to play that game, but at businesses instead of houses!

Christina Applegate

Very recently, I dreamed that I was making out with Christina Applegate. It was so cool, because she is so pretty, and has such a sexy cute little nose! In the dream, she and I were going to be together, but she had to run off and do a performance. She asked me, "One last thing before we go, can you please fix my plumbing?" There was an entourage waiting around really impatiently as I examined the plumbing. It took some work, but eventually I removed a few pieces that I wanted to have with me at the hardware store so that I could get compatible replacements.

Kristen Davis Dreams

I have had this exact same dream twice, over a year apart. Kristen and I are at a party after nightfall in someone's back yard. We are near a hedge in a poorly lit part of the yard. We both have a beer in a plastic cup, and we drink and talk. After a bit, we are flirting and holding hands. Soon, we are kissing. Then I wake up. Most of my dreams don't go much farther than that.

In another dream, I was in an entryway outside an auditorium. Kim Catrall and Kristen Davis were sitting on a bench next to each other talking. Kristen was on my right. I approached them, and I don't remember what was said, but I put my hands on Kristen's legs, just above her knees. I leaned in to my left and kissed her on her right cheek, and then woke up. I don't know what it means; a lot of these kissing dreams are really simple.

Debra Messing

I dreamed about being with Debra Messing on MIU campus, and walking with her near the pods. There was an Italian restaurant in this area, and we waited forever for a meal that never came. We walked back to her room and made out on the bed. We rolled off of the bed and, both naked, I started going down on her. The weird part of this dream is that her labia majora were shaped like Brazil nuts!

Hillary Clinton

This is one of the weirdest dreams ever! In this dream, I was at some party for Democratic big wigs, and Hillary Clinton was there. I have always respected and admired Hillary, and it is not surprising this in this dream we ended up kissing, in an intimate manner. The strange part is that in this dream, she was not married to Bill; she was married to George W. Bush! George somehow found out that I made out with his wife, and sent five secret service dudes to snuff me out (at the party); I ended up kicking their asses entirely (I frequently have super human powers in dreams.) I find the irony of Hillary and George being married entirely bizarre and hysterical!

Fucking Chick

I had this dream just a few months ago: I was in bed with a pretty cute brunette, and having sexual intercourse with her. At the time, I didn't know that it was a dream. I was so surprised to be having sex that I actually said aloud to her, "I didn't expect to ever have sex again in this lifetime." I don't remember what she said, but she responded verbally. This is the disappointing thing about a nice dream like that: I woke up and realized that (as usual) it was *just* a dream!

Ashley and the Flying Queaf

Ashley is this girl who used to work at the Vet clinic. She is a force of nature! A goddess indescribable, her eyes are like nebular clusters in which stars are born! It is not surprising that I had a dream about her. In the dream, she actually kind of rejected me. We were in a dormitory hallway, near a staircase. Several men picked her up and started to carry her up the stairs. I followed, and about half way up the first flight, she did a mid-air acrobatic maneuver while still being carried. She flipped upside down and on her back with her legs spread and her pussy pointed straight at me (she was naked, by the way.) WHOOOSH! She then let out a very large emission of air which flowed out and blew strongly over my face and chest! I was a bit embarrassed, and didn't know how to react. I didn't want to embarrass her though, and came up with something to say to make it seem okay. With apparent sincerity, I said, "Mmmmmm! As fresh as a mountain breeze!"

Eating Cute Brunette

This was a weird experience: For a week or two, I had had recurring dreams about going down on women. As usual, I was disappointed every time I woke up. In one particularly memorable dream, I was in a movie theater in the corridor where the drinking fountain and the bathrooms are. I met two very cute girls in about their lower 20's. They were both wearing skirts. One was shorter than the other, had long straight brunette hair, and was amazingly pretty. I leaned her up against the wall in a nook between the drinking fountain and the bathroom, and on my knees I lifted her skirt. She was *not* wearing panties! I remember eating her pussy, and then sadly I woke up from the dream. The next day, my mother told me on the phone that my nephew had lost his virginity, and that he had had his first serious girlfriend ever for about a week. "I know…" I thought to myself.

www.ingramcontent.com/pod-product-compliance
Lightning Source LLC
Chambersburg PA
CBHW070224140626
46555CB00018B/1263